The Pains of April.

The Pains of April.

Frank Turner Hollon

[signed] 10/16/1999

Over The Transom Publishing Company, Inc.
FAIRHOPE

Over The Transom Publishing Company, Inc.
323 De La Mare Avenue
Fairhope, Alabama 36532
e-mail: info@overthetransombooks.com

Library of Congress Catalog Card Number: 99-65784
ISBN 0-9643727-3-8

Manufactured in the United States of America

Quality Printing by
Nall Printing
Fairhope, Alabama

Typeset in Book Antiqua

Cover design by Mary Lou Hyland
Author's photo by Chris John, London Photography
Book design by Sonny Brewer and Kyle Jennings

First Edition 1999
10 9 8 7 6 5 4 3 2 1

This book is dedicated to those who read it and feel the same way I felt when I wrote it.

The Pains of April.

Introduced by Robert E. Bell

I received the manuscript on a Wednesday and finished the book the same day. I could have sat down and written an introduction then and there, but I wanted a chance to think about it. *The Pains of April* is a remarkable book, and I wanted to give some consideration to why I think so. It is incredible to me that a writer as young as Frank Turner Hollon — twenty-six when he wrote it — could write so perceptive a book about the inner life of an eighty-seven year old man. Even if the author based his perceptions on the recounted memories of an elderly friend or relative, and took careful notes, so intimate and faithful an interpretation as in *The Pains of April* would be nonetheless extraordinary.

7

Mr. Hollon didn't stop his exploration of the prospects of what it's like to live to be old with the narrator; he included three other characters of varying ages in his hurdling of the age gap. The author has a fine ear for dialog, and his characters are entirely believable. Mr. Hollon puts the reader into the mind of someone at the end of his life with never-varying fidelity, not even slipping into occasional editorial comment, which must have been a temptation when one is reaching across such a difference in years.

For me to say this book is the account of an eighty-seven year old man in a rest home simply does not give much of an idea what to expect. It is not easy for me to tell another what this book is about. The author does work on a narrow canvas, which, in this case, strengthens the presentation.

By listing some of the things the book is *not* about, one can more effectively say what it *is* about. Although it is not a regional novel, the opening tells us that the rest home is on the Gulf Coast, but the locale could just as easily be Oregon or Maine. The book is not about illness, death, and dying. None of the characters ever mentions his infirmities or dwells on medications, subjects the elderly usually find irresistible.

The narrator does not, as one might suspect, spend a lot of time thinking about death. His greatest fear is being consigned to the back dining room, from which

The Pains of April.

people tend to disappear from time to time.

He has an interesting philosophy about things he reads in the paper. He is curiously nonjudgmental in his reports of events that make an impression upon him. There was a teenager who accidentally hanged himself in a sex act. There were the men who shot two hundred and fifty wild horses in Utah. In each case, the narrator's comments are telling, but not didactic. He mentions his legal practice once or twice, but doesn't dwell on it.

One strength of the book is that the narrator is no one in particular. He is just an ordinary man, an ex-lawyer, who has grown old. He has retained his mental capabilities, even if somewhat diminished by time. So this book is about an old man and his days and nights. Every new day is a kind of copy of the day before, and this running countdown must be dealt with. The narrator's daily thoughts and memories alone would not sustain this novel. It is through his associates that the book comes to life. It is surprising how the other characters are so quickly incorporated into the movement of the book, which then becomes almost at once a study of active and passive among the four principals.

The introduction of Weber is inspired. He is active and aggressive, taking pleasure doing things he is not supposed to do. His exact opposite is Gus Robinson, much younger, extremely inhibited, afraid, and very passive. The narrator stands between the two. Whereas the narrator dreads ending up in the back dining room, Weber couldn't care less and actually eats there when he feels like it. Weber, who believes he has gills, is ingenious in dreaming up challenges for his friends, most all of them forbidden at the rest home, from fishing trips to tattoos. Weber does these things for the hell of it, but carrying them out becomes something of a drama for the other men, and makes their run-on of days seem more tolerable.

The traditional novel has a central conflict that has to be resolved, bringing about change, for better or worse. The conflict in this novel, however, is almost subterranean. There is no hint that the patients have reason to dislike or complain about the management of the nursing home. One gets the impression that the narrator is not too crazy about his sister and his daughter. Without saying so, just as happy out of their lives, particularly his daughter's church-going world. He loved his wife and says so quite a few times and her dying was devastating to him.

Still, neither is carried to the level of central conflict in *The Pains of April*. Instead, with careful craftsmanship, Mr. Hollon compels the reader to feel the inexorable countdown of days, and the knowledge, though seldom enunciated, that one by one the four friends will die. When I started this book, reading about Thanksgiving at Grandmother's house, I thought I was in for another flabby run of family history. But my mood changed at once, and it was held for the rest of the book. The ending of the novel is stunning. The final sentence is spine-chilling in its appropriateness, and I wish I had written it. So few writers understand style any more, but Mr. Hollon does. *The Pains of April* is a beautiful book.

Robert E. Bell
Davis, California
Award-winning author of *The Butterfly Tree*

Solidify my soul like a hard sun-dried
brick which blisters and
cracks in the heat of the day.
And use my soul with the souls of many others
to build a fortress around the beating heart
of the mind of mankind.
And build it strong so as to protect our God,
the very conscience of our combinations.
And when the evil winds blow,
the rains pelt down,
and the insects carve out tracks,
help us to weather ourselves.

The Pains of April.

I'm trying to decide whether I wish everyone on Earth would live forever, or wish everyone on Earth would die this afternoon and go where they belong. But there are other things to think about. Like Thanksgiving. It is spring—and I don't know why—but I have put Thanksgiving in with the pains of April. My aunt's house smells like my aunt's house. There are three groups of people here. The ladies are all over the kitchen making noises and talking about each other and themselves and wanting desperately to get all their things said before it's too late. Divorces and deathbeds have taken away faces. Births and remarriages have filled the empty chairs. There's very little difference.

The men talk about hunting and sports whether they want to or not. They watch the women when they can. The women hardly ever watch the men. Then there are the dogs and children. They are interchangeable. My grandmother is in the back room dying.

On this day to give thanks I am told there are many things to be thankful for. It's true. I am thankful that I am not my grandmother. I am thankful these many years later that I am not married and unable to take care of the woman I once loved and the children who are wrapped around my conscience and sit at the bottom of the river strapped to my freedom. I am thankful that I have decided to live another day. And I am thankful that God has let me make this decision. I am thankful for saxophones and women's dresses. I'm only allowed to look at one of the women in the kitchen. Everyone is aware of this and I've been granted some kind of tacit permission. Lust and Thanksgiving are not allowed together. The Pilgrims tried to take care of that.

Every now and then someone will sneak out of the living room and go visit Grandma. My turn will come. I will know it by the way I'm looked at. Because I am a man, my time will come at a man's time. At 16, I don't feel like a man. I feel like kissing the girl in the kitchen. I won't get permission for that. I have permission to wish for it. I have permission to draw pictures in my mind with light touches of nakedness. Maybe bare shoulders would be allowable. Or a bra strap. Should I try to explain this to my uncle? Or should I just tell him once again about my extravagant lack of plans for the future? He says he wishes he was me.

I am handed a knife and asked to carve the turkey. It is the first time I have been asked to do this. It is intended to be a proud moment for me, a kind of reward for never going to jail or marrying a poor girl. Sometimes I'm not sure where I'd rather be. War is hell. It is almost time to go see my grandmother. I wonder if she is thankful for being alive or just thankful for not being dead. Some people have no sense of timing when it comes to dying. A cat finds a place and lets its heart stop beating. There is no fear. There are no questions neatly typed and folded to fit in your pocket. A cat is a cat.

My grandmother has the sheet up to her chest. She was always very nice to me. She liked how I was different from the others. She was disappointed and pleased at the same time. She knew I would be the last to go into her room. She always knew things like that even when she didn't know them. She always had plenty of time to know them later. She never ran from wolves. It is, for her, April in the middle of November. I expected her room to smell like I expected it to smell. But there is almost no smell at all. She has the TV and her Bible to keep her awake. All her life she has been waiting to know when she would die. She could not stand the thought that a simple accident might crush her bones, denying her the chance to go slowly and deliberately. There just isn't enough time to get to know everyone the way they deserve to be known. We spend so much of the day on ourselves.

When I left my aunt's house at the end of that Thanksgiving Day, I never saw my grandmother again. She died five months later of the disease she hoped would kill her. She left me a matching set of souvenir spoons she had bought in New York. One of them had the Empire State Building engraved on the handle. I cannot remember what was on the other.

April 2

R ememembering Thanksgiving makes me remember a dream I had. The dream came only once, but with a clarity that makes me blink. I can still see the wolves.

There is nothing left but instincts. I can see nothing besides what is in front of me and hear nothing but what is behind me. The rain is pouring down in drops the size of my heartbeats. I am only minutes away from being killed and eaten by wolves or slipping away into the wet shadows to wait for the new day. There is very

The Pains of April.

little difference. April will continue with or without me. The wolves are very good at what they do. Fear has me hearing and smelling things that usually go unnoticed. Everything becomes important. There is no decoration, no waste, no extra time. Every step, every decision is essential. Wolves don't spend time wondering about right and wrong. They are always right. Wolves can't climb trees. There is weakness in every strength, and there is strength hidden in every weakness. The way my fingers are made to grasp and hold allows me to climb into trees. Every muscle in my body working together with perfect precision cannot outrun a wolf. But I can climb a tree. I cannot use my claws to break flesh. But I can climb a tree. And I can use my mind to figure out that a wolf cannot. These are weapons.

The wolves circle the bottom of the tree. The game has changed. The new weapon is patience. It is a virtue that must be waited for. The time in the tree is my reward for not falling down during the run or forgetting my situation for a second. Sometimes I'm not sure where I'd rather be. The wolves now know they cannot climb my tree. They didn't think about it until it was time to try: this approach lessens their pain and frustration. But not their hunger. Should I feel guilty because they are hungry? Don't be ridiculous.

When the sun came up, the wolves had gone. I desired food and water and sleep and sex. No words, just

17

desires. No explanations, just a drive to fulfill, to end the desires. Next time there may not be a tree to climb. Next time may be the last time. Knowing this, should I just live in the tree forever? Or never sleep again?

April 3

I have been in this rest home for seven months. I have a poor sense of timing when it comes to death. I got it from my grandmother. I can think of thousands of times when I should have died. Most of the people I used to picture coming to my funeral have died themselves.

I have a roommate. His name is Weber. He must have been a remarkable man once. I sometimes see flashes of brilliance in his nearly blind eyes. He has grown old, but he hasn't lost his sense of humor or his lust. He was caught last week in Mrs. Miller's room with his head between her legs. I think he got more pleasure from the reactions of the volunteers than he got from anything he did with Mrs. Miller. She's older than rocks. Which excuses them both.

Weber always talks about the big escape we'll make. Both of us are still allowed to eat in the front dining room. There are two dining rooms. The front dining

The Pains of April.

room is for the people who are still able to control their minds, or at least their mouths, and their bladders. The rear dining room is for those who have become physically incapacitated or who can no longer keep their train of thoughts on the rails. In here it is dangerous to have too much fun. It is dangerous to show too much of your personality. It is dangerous in here to say things before you think about them. The line is thin. In my seven months I have seen only one person fall back into the rear dining room and then catch herself often enough to be allowed back up front. I don't like to go back to the rear. I don't like to look there. I am afraid that one day I will forget how to die, and I will find myself back there being fed like a child.

Weber is allowed to stay in the front dining room with me. I am surprised they allow him this after some of the things he has done. But he is a fluid thinker. He can speak so softly and rationally sometimes I believe things from him that I know are not true. His daughter sometimes sneaks him a little Scotch. We stay up late and sip out of paper cups with the lights down very low. It was one of these nights that gave him the spark to go down to Mrs. Miller's room. It is on those nights that I think of my wife. She died a long time ago. I was only thirty. At first I felt sorry for myself. After a while I realized how her death had set me free. She was the only irresistible thing that I could not resist. I was almost never in love with her when we were together, and I was almost always in love with her when we were apart.

I knew the day she died that I would never be married again. I never was. I couldn't settle for less. Anything but boredom. Anything. Even hate. She was purples and golds and sharp edges. She made me stand on bridges with my heart held out in my hands, and she made me listen until I heard it splash into the rivers. No one else could satisfy me the way she couldn't. The day of her funeral I knew that I would be able to love the idea of her forever.

Marriage runs against me. I always felt that somehow it was a compromise, less than the best I could possibly be. To settle on one person is to give up on finding someone who makes you just a little bit happier, to give up on finding someone who makes you a tiny bit better at being alive. I only married her because I had no choice. I had to have her. That was all. I wouldn't change any of it. What's the point? In the long run there can be no right or wrong choices, only the choice I made and the choices I didn't. It's like going back years later and changing the words of a poem. When a poem is written it is written with the emotions and energy of that moment. To change even a few words is to lose the emotions and the energies that may be felt again only through the push and pull of the words on the page.

The Pains of April.

Like the push and pull of the words that wore the ink from this typewriter ribbon.

April 5

It is April 6. I hear the match light in the bathroom. Weber is sitting in there smoking a cigarette. He probably did the same thing in high school. We talked last night about getting old. I always swore I wouldn't live past thirty. When I turned twenty-eight I decided to push it back to forty. The next thing I knew I was seventy. Tomorrow I will be eighty-six. The toilet flushes and Weber brushes his teeth. It will not be long before he is moved to the back dining room. He believes that if you build a better guillotine the world will use it to cut off your head.

When they executed Gary Gilmore in Utah they put a bag over his head and a paper target on his chest. He was shot in the heart. He donate his eyes to someone who needed them. Gary Gilmore really only lived for those few moments — for the eternity — between the pull of the triggers and the bullets burying themselves in his chest.

April 6

It's all really pretty stupid. My daughter brought her grandchildren in for a visit this morning. Betsy can be a beautiful woman. She reminds me of my sister. Weber winks at me when she turns her back. He acts like we have some big secret that nobody else knows about. The only secret I know about is who killed John F. Kennedy. If you're six feet tall, you can't stand on the bottom of a seven-foot pool and still breathe. Weber believes he has gills. He tells stories about staying underwater for impossibly long periods of time. If it weren't for Weber, gray-green mold would grow on my stone face. He makes me change my expressions.

I used to think my eyes were only for seeing. Now I know that my eyes are also for other things. They are for smelling and hearing and tasting and touching. They are for imagining and wondering and picking out the real stars from the unreal. They are for catching fish and feeling the cold winds break through the trees and race across the open fields. My eyes are anything they see and everything they don't. My eyes are infinity times two when they are open. And even more when they are closed.

The Pains of April.

I used to be able to see myself perfectly. Now I peek around corners trying to catch a glimpse of my own head. I stand in front of the mirror and stare at my own grandfather. I've lived for eighty-six years, and now I'm nearly as helpless as the day I was born. It's some kind of social masturbation, futility in circles, rare moments when a man's weaknesses aren't weaknesses at all.

I remember when my sister died. I got a call from Lisa early one morning. I hadn't seen my sister in nearly three years. When you're a kid you can't imagine being away from your mother or father or sister for more than a few hours. But then I got older and the world got between us. It pushed us far apart. She was always alone. She and her husband gave up on the sanctity of marriage about eight months after they swore to love each other forever. Mom and Dad hadn't seen Lisa since the Christmas she got drunk and slept under the Christmas tree.

She called to say she was going into the hospital for a few days down in New Orleans. She acted like it was no big deal. It even sounded as if she simply wanted an excuse to call her big brother. I had always liked her, but that may be because I never knew her. I left work early and drove down to the hospital. No wonder they pay doctors so much money. They have to work in hospitals all day with sick people. I don't like hospitals. I don't understand the diseases and problems that make

23

these people look so weak and scared.

Lisa was in room 216. When I came through the door I could see that she was in a room made for two. A brown curtain was pulled between the beds. Lisa was asleep. She had already had some kind of operation. There were several machines around her bed. The plasma bag hung where I had pictured it hanging. Neither patient had visitors.

I sat down in the chair next to Lisa's bed. It was the only chair in the room. The old lady in the other bed stirred every now and then. The room smelled almost like urine, but not really. I couldn't place the smell.

I just sat there. Nurses came in every now and then, but they never spoke, and for different reasons I never asked any questions.

I thought about so many things. I thought about how beautiful Lisa had been when she was in high school. She was still beautiful. Her hair was blacker than midnight. Her eyes were closed, but I knew that behind her lids were dark brown eyes that could always make my eyes turn away before hers. She was a different girl. I suspect she was much smarter than I ever was. She seemed to see things in ways that I could not. She liked things that bored me, and she was bored with things that I found important. We were never close.

For hours I sat in that chair and thought with the clarity that can come only from silence and necessity.

The Pains of April.

Lisa never moved. I could see her heartbeat on the electric machine across from her bed. The old lady rustled around. I didn't want to look at her, so I didn't. Old sick people make me as nervous as newborn babies.

I thought about my wife. I thought about my job that I pretended to hate. Sometimes I did hate it. Usually only while I was there. I always had the weird feeling that my wife was going to move out while I was sitting at work one dull day filing my nails and listening to the phone ring. In a way I always hoped for her sake that she would find enough courage in the bottom of a sink full of dirty dishes to go away and look for life. And then Lisa died. I knew it even before I saw the line on the machine go flat across the screen. Her face never changed. It was more a feeling than anything I could see or hear. I just sat there. I didn't move. I didn't cry. It happened so fast. My little sister had died, and no one seemed to care. I walked out the door and drove home. There was nothing else to do.

April 12

I've discovered that there are two different ways to move from the front dining room into the rear. You can get pushed through the door in your favorite wheelchair, knowing exactly what is happening, but never catching anyone's eye. Or you can stumble in without the embryo of an idea and never spend another moment wondering why. I prefer the second. It's cleaner. It's a bullet point blank and perfect out the back. It's a bottle of sleeping pills and a good night's sleep. Doesn't anyone realize that there are a thousand other deaths besides the one that sends us to the grave? Doesn't anyone besides me see how much more painful and final these other deaths can be? Maybe Weber is right. Maybe my linear and disciplined way of thinking is my greatest enemy. He says that a house without windows isn't a house at all, it's a prison. He doesn't say the opposite. He doesn't say a prison with windows is a house. It's still just a prison.

Tuesday is Weber's birthday. He'll only be eighty-three. He wants a big cake with a girl inside. In all my life I've never been to a party that had a cake with a girl in it. I went to a party once that had a belly dancer. She had a rhinestone in her bellybutton. I had never seen a woman move with such stranded purpose. I could only watch her for a few seconds at a time. When the party was over, I kept the rhinestone. Years later my daughter swallowed it, and we had to take her down to the hospital.

Weber says the only way to really tell how old a woman is to cut her in half and count her rings like across a tree stump. This morning when I woke up he was sitting at the window in his Hawaiian shirt with his binoculars around his neck and his LSU baseball cap turned around backwards on his head. He called me over to the window because he said there was a herd of buffalo walking up the driveway.

April 27

When I was twenty-five years old, I got a job at a law office. I fell in love with the back of a woman's head in court one day. She ended up being my wife. I knew that if I stood still in one place too long I'd end up growing roots out the bottoms of my shoes. There were so many things I wanted to do. There were so many places I wanted to go. But I stood there anyway. And the roots grew. And when it was time to take the next step, it was too late, or too early — I don't know. Everyone has to have something or someone to think about in those moments lying in bed at night before your body decides to go to sleep. For so many years I used to think about the weird places I would like to go and the people who would live in these places. Then things took the places of those things, and in only a few months I was someone else lying awake at night thinking about something else.

Mostly I thought of situations. I pictured the funeral of every person close to me. I've pictured my own funeral so many times that it has become a separate memory. Sometimes I die in a car wreck. Sometimes I'm shot. Once I died in a parachute accident. People would come to my grave and cry for hours. It really wasn't until I was much older that it occurred to me that when I do finally die I will not get to see all these people come, and see them get down on their knees, and cry in the middle of the night.

The closest I ever came to dying was when I was about thirty-five years old. I got drunk in Santa Fe, New Mexico, and tried to break into a pet shop. I was bitten by a snake and woke up in the hospital with a headache that extended down my backbone and into the bowels of my soul. My only visitors were a deputy sheriff with a harelip and a friend of my mother's who lived in town and made the worst cookies I ever tasted. I shoved most of them under the mattress. I don't remember her name.

Sometimes I wake up in the middle of the night and Weber is standing at the window. He loves to tell the nurses that he sleeps naked. It isn't true. He slaps and winks when he says it, but sometimes I can see that he wishes he understood the love he has for life. We spend so much time perfecting the absence of emotion. That perfection is indifference. Indifference is man's greatest sin. Indifference is a hollow evil. Indifference is a perversion of emotion. Indifference is a mockery and sacrilege to the human spirit. When all you can see in the eyes is nothing, there is nothing to react to. There is nothing to pray for, nothing to desire, nothing at all left to do. The opposites of love and happiness aren't hate and sadness; the opposite of love and happiness is indifference. It is a weapon over which no one should gain control. I saw it in the eyes of the people in the rear dining room when I passed by this morning. I hope I never see it in the mirror.

(I wish sparks would fly from the saliva that slides from the old men's mouths and drips slowly down to their shirts. That their gray hair would glow in the dark like a science fiction movie. That old women's dresses would wave like wild sheets in a typhoon. I wish the smells of urine were a thousand trombones beating on the drums in my ear. That worn-out slippers were shiny metal spurs and elongated prison expressions. Wrinkles could be millions of miles of highways across an ocean of endless America. Tired eyes can become next year's crops and last year's litter of golden puppies. The green walls — they don't have to be walls at all. They can become wide-open spaces. Vast, unnecessary, century-old caverns of iridescent yellows and Scandinavian blues. Or popcorn, or the first night of the circus, or an empty casket, or a young man sitting at the table in the corner with his eyes tangled around the body of the girl sitting in the recesses.

The moans become the soothing sound of the ocean waves breaking one by one onto the beach. The whitecaps fall over and stretch up the sand like an old man's fingers reaching for a young man's strength. If broken down into the bare and basic elements, it is all really very ordinary. If dissected and picked apart piece by piece, the parts are only as complex as they are simple. Folds of loose skin could cover up a generation of harmless intentions. Or they could just hang there the way they do.)

April 27

The Pains of April.

I need to get Weber a birthday present. He wants a safari hat. I don't know where to get a safari hat. He told me yesterday that a safari hat is the only thing he has ever really wanted. For as long as he can remember he has wanted a safari hat. When he tells me these things, he looks me square in the eye and never smiles. He usually leaves me standing there without a clue as to whether or not he is serious. Why would anyone desire a safari hat for more than a few minutes? Maybe he saw one in a movie.

Tomorrow is the birthday party. April is almost gone away. When you are very old, there is a constant fear that everything that happens is happening for the last time. I will call my daughter and have her buy a safari hat. How much does such a thing cost? I might have her buy two safari hats.

April 28

I t's taken almost my entire life to realize that people like Weber have something that people like me don't. I have always had an overwhelming desire to be somebody. I want some sort of immortality. I want people to think about me after I'm dead. For as long as I can remember, I've always wanted to be someone else. Sometimes it's a famous person, sometimes it's just a guy sitting across the restaurant with a glass of wine in one hand and the world in the other. Weber has never wanted to be anyone but himself. He doesn't want anyone to cry at his funeral, and he says he is looking forward to his bones decomposing and going back to the soil. I can't decide whether he is ahead of me or behind me.

Is no one any better or any worse than anyone else? Maybe Weber believes this is true and it is the reason he isn't afraid to die. I have been afraid of dying every day of my life. I have been philosophically afraid of dying as well as afraid of the pain. I have been afraid of the idea of death and all the little things that go along with it. I have never liked people who said things that didn't fit neatly into the conversation. I always wanted to be those people, but I never really liked them.

April 29

We sang "Happy Birthday" four times. Weber's nineteen-year-old retarded granddaughter sat and listened, as beautiful and detached as an angel in a cage. She smiled at me and meant nothing. I smiled back and tried to do the same.

We wore birthday hats and ate store-bought cake. When Weber opened my birthday gift, he was happier than anyone I've ever seen. He acted like his new safari hat was the last puzzle piece and now he could relax. He never took that hat from his head the whole day. I left mine under the bed. And fell asleep thinking that if I had given Weber a pair of shoes, he might have been just as happy. Or a walking cane. Or a book, or a beer, or nothing at all.

April 29

When I woke up, Weber was already out of bed and gone to breakfast. I washed my face and combed my hair and brushed my teeth. I put on a shirt and blew my nose on a towel. My slippers were under the bed next to the safari hat. I pushed the hat aside. Sunshine peeked around the side of the curtain.

I closed the door behind me when I left the room. Sometimes I feel like a character in a book. A character who doesn't really make decisions because everything is already written.

To get to the front dining room I have to pass by the entrance to the rear dining room. I always look. When I looked this morning I stopped in the doorway. The first thing I saw was a safari hat. Weber was sitting at a table in the corner. He was being fed by one of the young girls. I could see his eyes. They were still very blue. I could see his hands folded in his lap. He looked older. Mr. Finch sat across the table talking to himself and stirring his food round and round. I have never known him to do anything else.

Seeing Weber in the rear dining room made me feel sick in my stomach. It made me wish for things I had hoped I would never wish for. At first it made me hate the world. Then it made me hate Weber. And then he saw me. He didn't hesitate. In one fluid movement he smiled very slowly and winked.

I guess that was the first moment I realized everything would be okay. It was in that single moment that I began to feel at ease. It didn't matter why Weber was in the rear dining room. It didn't matter whether he was there against his will or because he was smarter than everyone and had tricked his way into some sort of heaven. It didn't matter that he would never be allowed into the front dining room again. The things that really mattered were already taken care of. Even at the end of April there are so many things to learn.

April 30

I woke up this morning to see Weber sitting next to my bed. He had his fingers to his lips and his safari hat pushed back on his head. Since Weber has gone I've gotten a new roommate. His name is Robinson. He is a younger man who stays mostly to himself all day and talks in his sleep at night. Sometimes he whispers to someone named Julia. Sometimes he screams about guns. And sometimes he talks to God. When I listen very carefully to hear God talk back, I never hear anything. I hear train whistles and thunder. I hear my own heartbeat and the air being pulled into my body and pushed out again. I hear lots of things, but I never hear God speak out loud to Gus Robinson.

"How come you don't talk to me any more?" Weber asked.

I wanted to tell him he was wrong, but he wasn't. Since he had been moved out I had not spoken to him one time. Even though he was moved to the west wing, I would still see him nearly every day.

"I'm no different, you know."

He didn't seem different. When I would see him across the courtyard he would tip his hat or point to one of the ladies and smile. I think I was different.

Weber was speaking very softly. He didn't want to wake Gus Robinson. Neither did I. If you left him alone, he would stay alone all day, but if you started a conversation about anything at all, in a few grueling minutes he would be telling you about his days in the stock market, or his investment strategies, or Swiss bank accounts, or something called the Cherokee Code. He had been very successful once. He had scars on his wrists to prove it. They went from top to bottom instead of side to side. One early morning I woke up before he did and looked at those scars for a long time. I pictured him in the bathroom of a large house, sitting on the floor in a tuxedo with his back against the tub and a bottle of bourbon leaning against his leg. He was in his early forties, handsome, and had everything. With nothing left to want, he had no reason to get out of bed in the morning. No reason to believe that life could ever get any better. He didn't slice open his arms for attention. He did it because he wanted to die. He woke up disappointed the next day and spent the rest of his life ashamed of the disappointment.

"Let's go fishing."

"What?"

"Let's go fishing," Weber repeated.

"We can't go fishing."

"We're grown men. If we feel like going fishing, we'll go fishing. There's a pond in the woods in the back."

"How do you know there's a pond in the woods in the back?" I asked.

"Because there's a pond in the woods in the back," he answered.

I knew there had to be some kind of reason we couldn't just get up and go fishing. If I thought long enough, I could find the reason why we couldn't just get up and go fishing.

"We don't have fishing poles."

"Yes, we do."

Gus Robinson rolled over and said, "What about bait?"

If Weber hadn't wanted Gus Robinson to go fishing with us, he never let it show. He answered as if Gus Robinson had been in the conversation all along.

"We've got crickets."

"Crickets?"

"Crickets."

We went fishing.

After my wife died, I used to take my little girl fishing. I wanted Betsy to be everything. I wanted her to be my son, my daughter, my friend, and my wife. She wanted me to be everything. Neither one of us ever measured up. I finally learned from Betsy not to expect too much from people.

When we would catch a fish, she would take it from the hook and drop it back into the water. She was never afraid. She would tell me that fish were meant to live in water. It wasn't wrong to kill a fish for food, but it was wrong to take it from the water for too long. Through a million years God helped the body of a fish to change until it could breathe in water. Gills and scales came from lungs and skin, she said. Every time we took a fish from the water we were worshiping the wrong god, she said. Every time we took a fish from the water, she said, we were wasting millions of years of wisdom and perfection in only a few seconds.

Betsy is married now and lives in Louisiana. She has three children. She and her husband haven't missed a Sunday church service in twenty-two years. One Sunday their house burned to the ground while they were in church. My daughter believes it was a miracle. She believes that if they had been home they would all have been burned alive. The fire started because somebody left the stove on.

We fished for most of the day. Gus Robinson told stories about catching hundreds and hundreds of fish. Weber told stories also. His stories had to do with sitting in a boat all day drinking beer and pissing over the sides. He never mentioned how many fish they caught. He told us he had the ability to breathe under water because his mother was as big as a whale. Gus Robinson looked at Weber out of the corners of his eyes.

I was afraid that if I was caught out there they would make me eat in the rear dining room with Mr. Finch. Every time I started to leave, Weber threatened something I knew he wouldn't do. He said everything had been arranged.

From where I sat I could see the scars stretch up Gus Robinson's upper arms and run directly along the angle of the fishing pole. They continued the length of the pole, stopped at the top, and raced down the thin fishing line to the place where the line goes under the water. Gus Robinson turned his wrist and looked at the hard skin. I could see his face. When he looked at the scars, he saw everything. He stared at his wrist like it was a movie. He could probably still feel the blade touch base and slide through his skin. He could probably close his eyes and feel the warm blood soaking through the bottom of his pants from the cool tile of the bathroom floor. It's more real now than the day it happened.

He must still feel the adrenaline that we once needed to run a step faster and dig our claws one millimeter deeper. The same adrenaline we used playing tackle football at the park. My daughter would have sat in the boat and said that wasting adrenaline is the same sin as taking fish from the water. She would have smiled and said God gave us that adrenaline for a purpose. I would have smiled back, suppressing the desire to scream at God for making my daughter have any conception of purposes at eight years old. At that age she should have been color-blind and double-jointed and wondering why Saturdays don't feel like Wednesdays. She should have been taking apart flashlights to see how they work. When she was eight years old, she asked me at breakfast one morning if we could take apart the dog.

Things get so complicated. When I was young I remember thinking that older people must surely have everything figured out. They all seemed so calm and prehistoric. They had answers for every question I could dream up. I never imagined that they had new questions. It never occurred to me that there was no end.

The Pains of April.

The fish Gus Robinson caught reminded me of a girl I once knew. It was small, with a big head. The top fin stuck straight in the air. Its lungs heaved in and out when it was taken from the water. The cricket on the end of the hook had been pushed up the line. It was too big to fit in the mouth of the fish. How could a fish make such a mistake? Weber clapped his hands and laughed. Gus Robinson pulled the hook gently from side to side until it slid from the lip. He looked at the fish very closely and smelled it. He touched the points on the top of the fin with his index finger. Then he dropped the fish back into the water.

We sat awhile. Weber smoked. Gus Robinson stared at the cork floating on top of the pond. His scars still stretched from his wrists up the fishing pole and down the line into the water. For all I knew they continued straight into the core of the Earth, like roots.

He took a long breath and started to say something. Weber and I waited for the story about the time Gus Robinson turned money into more money. Or the time he zigzagged and bluffed and outsmarted and sat co-agulated on a park bench made out of gold and emer-alds and tiny pieces of the sun. We waited for tales of riverboats and naked angels and kings and queens who had too much to drink and gave away secrets that no one should know.

Instead he said, "I don't think there's another fish in

this pond. I think I caught the only fish in this whole damned pond."

Weber said, "Then catch him again."

July 23

I remember the things Mr. Bailey used to tell me. He was a black man who worked for my father. After my mother and father died, Mr. Bailey worked for me. He always looked the same. His eyes were always red, and his hands were always the hands of a man who worked hard. I always picture Mr. Bailey standing or sitting alone.

He had no brothers or sisters. He had no wife, and he had no children. He could fix anything that broke, and he could smile at anything I said.

I think of him as an old man, but he was really only ten years older than me. I never saw him drunk, but when I was a boy, Mr. Bailey used to sit out on the porch with my father and drink homemade whiskey. When I was raising my daughter alone in that big house, Mr. Bailey would come by with a jar of whiskey, and we'd sit in the living room late at night with the doors and windows open. Some nights we'd sit for hours and say nothing. It was never uneasy. Sometimes we'd talk and laugh, and I'd end up spilling myself all over this black man's hands.

On a particularly hot night in the middle of a Mississippi summer we sat with the fan propped up against the screen door. My daughter was somewhere upstairs stuck to her sheets. So many nights I'd sat in that house and told Mr. Bailey things about myself that I didn't even tell myself. Mr. Bailey would just listen and nod his head and smile genuinely in the right places. He never talked about himself.

On this one night I asked Mr. Bailey why he never got married. He told me that all his life he had watched people held hostage by things they loved. He watched people build their own prisons and then wonder how they got inside them. People who loved money were crazy for more of it. People who loved other people would do anything to stay right alongside them. His list went on forever. Some people sacrificed for lust, some for stardom, some for religion. But whatever it was, for Mr. Bailey it was a mistake to make the sacrifice. He said he didn't know everything about love, but he knew it had to be an addition, not a subtraction.

I realized that night how scared Mr. Bailey really was. I was forty-one years old, and Mr. Bailey was fifty-one. The world had done things to him that had made him afraid. It wasn't a burden for him to listen to me on those drunk nights. He loved hearing my fears. His heart got to stay in his chest while mine sat on the living room table on one of my mother's white china plates.

July 24

Some situations are stone-cold stupid. Like walking around in that woman's room in the middle of the night dressed like the Tooth Fairy trying to steal her virginity out from under the pillow. She should have known I wasn't capable of keeping the promises I made. She should have seen that I was the vulnerable one. I was the one who stood naked on the railroad tracks with my eyes closed and my fingers in my ears. I can't always be the one to make sense of things. It isn't natural. It isn't healthy. I won't apologize for letting the world get out of hand. I can't protect all the people who can't protect themselves. It isn't my responsibility. Cut me and I bleed. Feed me and beat me and leave me sprawled in my own feces. How long does a person have to feel guilty for taking advantage of another person?

I needed her and she was there. She needed to be needed. People want things guaranteed to last forever. People want situations captured and held perfectly still like in a photograph. Captured and reliable and one-dimensional. It has nothing to do with poetry. It has to do with being afraid. It has to do with the illusion of thinking you can possibly know where you will be—or *should* be—five years from now.

She would say, "Tell me you love me."

And I would say, "I love you."

She would say, "Tell me you'll always love me."

And I would say, "I love you."

It wasn't a lie. I loved her in that moment. I told her I loved her because I loved her. Maybe I wouldn't love her ten minutes later, and maybe I hadn't loved her ten minutes before, but I loved her the moment I told her I loved her. She could never understand that. I never really understood it myself. My wife taught me a lot of things. Not all of them were good. The women who came along after she died learned to believe in ghosts.

I'm eighty-six years old, and I honestly can't remember the last time I kissed a woman. I can't remember how good it felt or how exciting it was to finally push myself up against her. I've forgotten the clean exhilaration when your hand slides under her dress and you know it won't be long. To lie naked in the bed with something you desire so much your entire body can shake. Something you desire more than food or water or a reason to live. It used to make me hate myself. I used to hate the way she would smile up at me when she knew I couldn't control myself.

If I do not eat, I will die. If I do not sleep, I will die. If I do not breathe, I will die. My body telegraphs its desires to my brain. It is my mind's job to understand and control my desires. This is the thing that truly separates me from the wolves. When a wolf is hungry, he eats. When he is tired, he sleeps. When he is sexually excited, he has sex. That is all there is to it. It isn't a decision. A man's body should only make suggestions. Then his mind should take over. A wolf cannot give himself these choices. A wolf is a wolf.

"I had a dog once."

"What kind of dog was it?" I asked. We were sitting in my room drinking hot Scotch from Dixie cups. Gus Robinson was taking off his shoes. Weber was talking about his dog.

"It was a real dog. The kind of dog that knocks over the neighbor's garbage and shits wherever he feels like taking a shit."

Gus Robinson pulled off the second shoe and dropped it on the floor. He smelled the hot Scotch and took a sip. He shook his head and said, "How the hell did you manage that fishing trip, Weber?"

He didn't really wait for an answer before he said, "Three old men just aren't allowed to walk out the back door of this place and go fishing without some kind of special arrangement."

Weber laughed and said, "One night, past midnight,

that damned dog started barking and whining like the Devil himself was sitting in the back yard drinking a Coca-Cola. I got up when I couldn't stand it any more and went out back with my flashlight in one hand and a baseball bat in the other. In the middle of the back yard was a big oak tree. The closest branch came out of the trunk of the tree about ten feet above the ground. I'll be damned if that dog wasn't sitting up in that tree with his tail between his legs and the wildest look on his face. I don't know if he was glad to see me or if he was embarrassed to be a dog in a tree."

Weber waited a few seconds, took his first sip from the Dixie cup, and said, "Anyway, when I finally got him down, he was so excited he pissed all over himself. I don't know to this day how that dog got into that damned tree. It never happened again."

Weber tipped the safari hat to the back of his head and raised the paper cup to his lips. Gus Robinson just sat across the room and stared at him. He didn't ask any more questions. I think he was mad at himself because he enjoyed Weber's story about the dog.

July 25

47

Maybe I'll get up in the morning. Maybe I won't. Maybe I'll drag my old dead body out of bed. Maybe I'll just stay in bed. I learned I wasn't a painter because I tried to paint. I learned I wasn't a great hunter when I shot a deer in Alabama. I didn't have to eat a bowl of shit to know I wouldn't like it. I didn't have to sit in my tuxedo on the cold bathroom floor to know that I didn't have whatever it takes to cut my wrists from top to bottom. There were times when it didn't seem like such a bad idea. Mr. Bailey would tell me that middle age was the hardest time in a man's life. It was the time when you began to question all the myths. It was the time when you had a chance to stop and see just exactly where you weren't going. Thousands of years ago people used to die before they ever reached our middle age, before they had a chance to feel ridiculous.

My hair is still falling out. I thought by now it would all be gone. I was always proud of my body. I was proud of the speed of my reactions and the belief that my body would allow me to survive even if my mind gave up. But now it is my mind that keeps me alive. I don't see so good any more. Weber says it's just as well because

The Pains of April.

I don't look so good any more anyway, and if my eyes were perfect I'd be depressed all day after the morning shave.

I still don't like walking past the rear dining room every morning. I don't like hearing Weber's voice or getting a glimpse of that stupid hat. Today it made me think about something I read in the newspaper. Two men on snowmobiles sat up on an American mountain side in Utah with high-powered rifles and a bottle of whiskey. They shot two hundred and fifty wild horses down in the valley below. Two hundred and fifty carcasses were found in the snow with bullets resting inside. To kill for food is to survive. To kill for hate is human. To sit on a mountain side and kill horses from a distance is a separate evil. It is too separate for me to understand.

July 30

Yesterday morning I couldn't remember the address of the house where I grew up and spent most of my life. I couldn't even remember the name of the street. I just sat there. Over and over I pictured myself and Mr. Bailey going from window to window nailing boards over the glass. I pictured Betsy in the kitchen with a box full of candles and matches, with cans of food and kerosene lamps. The wind was already high, and the sky told its story to people who had grown up all their lives on the Mississippi coast. We put the lawn furniture in the barn, along with anything else in the yard that could be blown by the wind.

People get excited when a hurricane is on the way. It's interesting to notice how different people react. Some people pay little attention at all. Some people run around in a panic like the world is coming to an end. It might be. There's something special about a hurricane. It's out of control. It does exactly what it feels like doing. Somehow it's closer to God. It can be strong and wicked, and then it can be gone. It doesn't ask permission. It doesn't apologize.

I would say, "Looks like a wild one, Mr. Bailey."

Mr. Bailey would answer, "Yes, sir, it does."

He could see how excited I would get. He could see how much I really enjoyed the crisis. With the wind and rain and lightning we would sit inside and listen for the snap and crash of pine trees and wait for the silence in the eye of the storm. We'd tell stories about fierce winds that blew cars from the road and sent branches through the belly of a cow.

I would drink too much and say things like, "Do you think we should go out and make sure the barn door hasn't blown open?"

Then I would wake up the next morning with my head hurting and the storm ended.

Drury Lane. The house is on Drury Lane. Eleven fifty-seven. It's the last house on the right before the road comes to a dead end. It's a blue two-story with an old oak tree in the front yard and big windows in the front. There's a screened-in porch and a chimney on the side. Almost always there's a dog in the front yard lying in the sun waiting for the postman. That house makes me feel good. It made me feel good to be there, and it makes me feel good to think about it. I wish I was there now. I wish I was sitting on the porch in the rocking chair on the hottest day of the year with my shirt full of sweat and a cold drink pressed up against the side of my face. I can feel the fan churning air around my chest. I can see Betsy outside on the swing talking to herself the way she used to and trying to understand puberty. If I would walk to the east window I could see the graveyard across the field where her mother is buried. But I won't get out of the chair. I won't take the drink from the side of my face, and I won't forget. It's one thing not to remember; it's another to forget.

August 4

51

I t's the way they can take a picture
and make it smaller and more detailed by pushing it into itself, form-
ing little wrinkles. My mother used to say,
"The young people will ask you to do things to make
them happy, and the old people will ask you not to do
things that make them unhappy."

This place where I am is the place where people
come to die. Elephants and Indians have burial
grounds. Birds try not to die in flight. Old America goes
to a rest home to die. People die here nearly every day.
They wait in their rooms with apology blisters all over
their tongues. They wait for action. Big action. They
space their shoes out in their closets and wipe off imagi-
nary dust. Shoehorns and ugly yellow sheets. A weird
place to die.

I found a chicken bone behind the television set. I
would rather find an arrow through my heart. My pajama top would have a spot of blood on the front. Maybe
the arrow would go right through an empty buttonhole.
If it went through a buttonhole, it might not rip my pajama top. It might go clean through and into my chest
without ruining my shirt. The steel arrowhead would

The Pains of April.

shatter my breastbone, and the point would push through into my heart. The heart would keep pumping and pumping with the steel tip about an inch inside. Blood would come out through the hole in my chest and stain my light-blue pajama top. If my heart kept pumping, the blood would keep pouring out through the hole. Pretty soon the blood would soak the sheets and drip over the side of the bed. Either my heart would stop pumping or I would run out of blood. The arrow would pulse with every heartbeat. The sharp tip would cut deeper every pulse. My heart would slowly cut itself to pieces, the way Gus Robinson tried to do. Maybe it's almost the same thing. Maybe life pushed Gus Robinson up against those razor blades the same way the arrow came crashing through my chest and stuck its head into the edge of my heart. Maybe every breath he took pressed the blades deeper and deeper into his wrists just like every pump of my heart ripped it more and more. The more I tried to survive, the worse it got. The harder it pumped, the more muscle was torn away.

August 17

I woke up this morning with a shot-gun pain coming from where I imag-ine my intestines to be. Through the window I saw them carry Mr. Finch out on a stretcher with a sheet pulled over his face. I didn't know it was Mr. Finch until someone told me later. When you're old you don't need a reason to die. You don't need to be run over by a truck or hit your head on the side of a pool. When you're old you can just die for no reason.

August 19

We sat in our underwear smoking ci-gars. The door was locked and the window was open because the air conditioner was broken. It ran, but only made a noise. Smoke floated up from the table and was sucked out through the window across the room.

The television was on, and there was a half-empty bottle of bourbon on the floor next to the wall. Weber dealt out the cards. We were only playing for nickels and dimes, but I had already lost eleven dollars. Gus Robinson kept glancing at the door as if the police were going to bust through any minute. Weber probably would have loved it. He stood up, walked across the room, and urinated out the window with his cigar hanging from his mouth and hair on his back.

Gus Robinson was always interested in who Weber knew to get permission for poker games and fishing trips. He believes in connections and contacts and the currency of advantage.

There was a fourth man at the table. His name was Sidney Painter. Sidney laughed at nearly everything Weber did. There was nothing fake about the laugh. He laughed because it was funny. Gus Robinson almost never laughed. He always thought there was something going on.

The television was talking about pregnancy. It was one of those new channels that can say and do things that couldn't be said or done. They showed a film of a Mexican woman having a baby.

Sidney said, "Isn't it amazing?"

"Isn't what amazing?"

"Having a baby. Isn't it amazing the way a baby can live inside of a woman for nine months? Then the baby squeezes out into the world. It must hurt like hell."

Gus Robinson looked over at the television screen and then back at Sidney.

Sidney shook his head. "None of us will ever know how it feels to have a baby."

Weber laughed and said, "I passed a kidney stone once. Does that count?"

Gus Robinson picked up his cards and looked back at the television. The Mexican woman had her feet up in stirrups. She was shaking her head from side to side. The doctor was saying something to her in Spanish. I started to get an erection. I leaned forward in my chair and tapped the ashes from the end of my cigar into a glass of water. At the beginning of the evening Weber made a rule that the player who lost the most money in the card game would have to drink the glass of water filled with ashes. Gus Robinson believed him. I saw Gus cheat once. I wondered if he cheated for the money or so he wouldn't have to drink the glass of ashes.

Sidney has a pointed face. He is a man who seems to understand himself. I believe that he is happy. He isn't afraid. He has nothing to prove.

Sidney lives down the hall. His wife lives with him. She has Alzheimer's disease and isn't able to take care of herself. Sidney does everything for her. He takes care of his wife the way the Mexican girl will take care of the screaming baby that comes from her body.

We stayed awake very late that night. I ended up losing nineteen dollars. Everyone else claimed they broke even. I saw Gus Robinson stuff a handful of change in his top drawer. I saw Sidney see him do it. I saw Sidney see Gus Robinson cheat earlier. I saw Gus Robinson look at Weber when he thought Weber wasn't looking, and I saw Weber look at his cards but see Gus Robinson looking at him from across the table. I thought to myself that if four old men playing cards in their underwear can be this complex, then there isn't a chance that we will ever figure out the world and nuclear energy and space and the stuff that makes our hearts keep beating.

August 29

I saw a big yellow cat jump up on the windowsill from outside. It was the end of August, and still very hot. The old air conditioner would kick on and off back and forth again and again.

"A person is irresponsible when he takes on responsibilities and commitments he can't live up to, to let other people rely on his promises and intentions. But, it isn't irresponsible to survey the situation, balance the benefits, and make a rational choice not to make certain commitments."

"It's a copout. You were afraid. You were afraid you

might not be smart enough or good enough. You chose to believe you were better than everyone else from the beginning. You were better than the people who worked hard to be someone."

"I was already someone."

"Who?"

"I was someone the day I was born."

"Is that the same thing as being confused?"

"There's nothing wrong with being confused. In fact, there may be something wrong with not being confused. I had a dream last night about an Australian girl. She was young. Real young. I can remember sitting in a house. It was more like a hut. There were two girls, sisters. One was sixteen and one was thirteen. I told the thirteen-year-old girl that I was too old for her. I told her it was wrong for me even to desire her. She shook her head and told me nothing was wrong unless we decided it was wrong. The next thing I knew we were standing in a hallway. She had her back to me, and her shirt was off. Her skin was dark, and my arms were wrapped around her from behind. When I woke up this morning I felt new and good and alive. I fell in love with a thirteen-year-old girl from Australia that doesn't even exist."

August 31

The Pains of April.

They must believe in bruises.
I hear people say all the time that they knew something was going to happen before it happened. I knew when my wife went to the hospital to have our second child that something wrong was about to happen. I stopped in front of the mirror and knew that years later I would see the scene again and know that I knew.

The first thing I noticed was the wind. It was in bullets. Little gusts would shoot around curves and come to a stop at the end of the telescope. Maybe it was my imagination. Maybe it was the way my wife would drink until she fell asleep on the couch with the cat curled up around the bags under her brown eyes. I knew there would be decisions to make. Black decisions. The kind without a ribbon. Wrapped in a plain paper bag.

"Open it."

"No."

"Open it."

It was my last present. I knew when I opened it that Christmas would be over. Then the world would try to convince me through the words of Tommy Barnes that there was no Santa Claus and there had never been a

Santa Claus. I didn't realize at the time what a blow to the head those words really were.

I finally opened my present. It was a hammer.

September 3

My mother used to lock me in the bathroom for hours and hours. Her nerves would fray into a slow evangelical screw. She was destined and damned to the chemical fluctuations of a woman. I was destined and damned to spend certain hours locked in the bathroom with a mouthful of silence and an umbilical cord of Teflon.

She would apologize as if she had beaten the future from the skin on my ass. I would almost feel guilty for thinking I deserved any apology at all. Being locked in the bathroom isn't so bad. There was just enough fear in my bloodstream to allow me to think faster and clearer than usual. The porcelain was cold and white, just like the thoughts that grew behind the locked door of that bathroom. During my middle-age anarchy I would sit alone in the dry tub with all my clothes on trying to steal the coldness and whiteness from the floor and walls.

Now, for some reason, it makes me think of Curtis

The Pains of April.

Bentley. He always carried a jackknife. Curtis Bentley sat in the front yard down the street and held his arm in an ant bed while we timed him. He held it there for five minutes, and we were glad to each give him the dollar we had promised. It was the best dollar I ever spent. Curtis claimed that ants won't bite unless they are given a reason to panic. Curtis was wrong. His arm was solid red. Six dollars wasn't enough to buy away the pain.

I never once looked at the stopwatch. From the beginning I stared directly at his face. The poison from the red ants made Curtis's face draw tight. Poison can be a marvelous thing.

September 17

I'm beginning to see things differently. I'm beginning to appreciate things I overlooked before. I fed my medicine to a squirrel on the windowsill this morning. I put it next to an acorn, and he ate both of them. He ate the acorn first. I thought for a moment he would leave the pill. He picked it up and put it down. The second time he picked it up he ate it. I saw myself standing at the window clapping. Gus Robinson was not in the room. Gus Robinson needs his ass kicked one good time. I've always heard people

61

say that, and I always wanted to be able to say it in front of a crowd of people. I have watched myself watch other people across rooms and restaurants and dinner tables. I have watched myself watch gestures and salutes and mating rituals that were grotesque enough to send the blood rushing to the big place. I have rehearsed and rehearsed a million lines for a million scenes with a million make-believe people. Weber would understand. He dedicated his life to being anything but me. He'd even rather be Gus Robinson than me. At least Gus Robinson has scars running up his wrists. I wonder if it is too late to be someone else. Is it too late to break down the individual cells and rebuild a completely separate chemical structure? Is it too late to smell different and taste different and say different things at different times? Would I be disappointed? Maybe I expected too much.

My daughter came to visit me this morning. She brought along the grandchildren. They always seem afraid. Betsy wears ugly clothes. I would never tell her, but she's always worn ugly clothes. In an interesting way she is beautiful. She is not a result of her mother; she is a reaction.

She asks questions and doesn't wait for the answers.

"Are they treating you right?"

"Are you comfortable?"

"Where is your hairbrush?"

The Pains of April.

I'm trapped inside an eighty-six-year-old wrinkled white body that listens to my mind at half-speed. My answer to each question comes in the middle of the next question. No wonder she doesn't wait. I cannot picture her naked. My underwear is riding up my crack, and my testicles are never comfortable in these new pants.

October 15

I **woke up last night for no reason.** The digital clock next to the bed showed 3:31 a.m. The air conditioner is fixed, but the window was open. It took me a minute before I could make out the figure of Gus Robinson in the dark standing in front of the mirror across the room. He stood there for a few moments before he reached over and switched on the lamp. When the light came up we were looking at each other in the mirror.

I asked him if everything was all right.

"Yes."

I asked him what he was doing awake at 3:30 in the morning.

He stared at himself in the mirror and then brought his face close against the glass.

"Do you see these rings under my eyes?" He didn't want an answer.

"These rings are from the day my wife left me. I got home from work one afternoon and she was gone. I talked to her on the phone the next morning. She called and said I deserved an explanation. She said she would answer any question I wanted to ask. I asked her why she left. She said she wasn't happy. I asked her if she still loved me. She said she wasn't sure she had ever loved me at all. I asked her where my favorite socks were. She said she didn't know. That was the last thing we ever said to each other."

I sat up in bed and watched every detail of Gus Robinson. There was something oddly calm about the way he was moving and the way his words came from his mouth.

"See these lines around my eyes?"

He ran his finger down the lines as if it were the first time he had taken a moment to touch his face.

"These lines are from the year I lost the family business. I started to feel indestructible. I didn't think I was capable of making a bad decision. Then I made five or six in a row."

I asked him what kind of business he had. He didn't answer.

His fingers gently traced the lines up to his eye and he said, "It takes centuries for a river to carve its riverbed through the mountains."

"Gus, why don't you get back in bed?"

The Pains of April.

He ran his hand through his hair and down the back of his head. When his hand reached the base of his neck, he stopped. I could see in the mirror that he was staring at the scars on his wrist. He lifted his left arm and turned his scars out so he could see both wrists in the mirror.

"It's 3:30 in the morning, Gus. Turn out the light and go back to bed."

With his open wrists turned toward the mirror he began to lift and spread his arms outward till they came to full extension. He would stare at one wrist for a few minutes and then shift his eyes to the other wrist. The entire episode lasted eighteen minutes. I looked back and forth from the clock to Gus Robinson. At 3:49 he dropped his arms and turned off the lamp. He crawled back into bed. I stayed awake wondering whether I would say anything to him the next morning or whether we would never speak about it. For such a simple thing it didn't seem so simple at all.

It has taken me a long time to learn to like Gus Robinson. Everyone has his own approach to the world, and a way he likes to be seen. Gus Robinson builds a wall around himself. Everything he says and everything he does is said and done with the wall in mind. He wants to be seen as successful and strong. He is on the playground with his chest stuck out and his hands drawn into fists. It isn't easy to like him. It isn't easy to care enough to see around his wall. It has taken me quite some time to learn how important it is to him that I take the time to understand; to understand that he has no choice. He wants me to see him behind his wall. Through gestures and words he has let me see that he is a good man. It is a constant effort. Sometimes it is worth it, sometimes not. When we are around Weber it is particularly tiresome. Gus Robinson isn't very comfortable with people who are comfortable.

Weber has reached a point where his weaknesses aren't really weaknesses. He's probably been at that point all his life. When you're around Weber it seems as if nothing is unspeakable, nothing is off-limits. He exposes himself until the people around him aren't afraid to be naked.

From the very beginning Weber tells stories and uncovers scars. He makes a point of letting you see his imperfections. Before I knew why, I was telling him secrets I thought were buried forever. He has a way of making most people feel alive. There is a trick to all this. No. It isn't really a trick. There is no malice. There is no pressure. In fact, I find that I want to tell Weber nearly everything.

When I was young I believed that everyone had nearly the same intelligence and capacity to learn. I don't believe that any more. Weber is smarter than I will ever be. He sees things that I will never see, the same way

The Pains of April.

that a true pool player sees shots on the table that never cross my mind. Weber is his own god. It is amazing that he has survived so long in this kind of world. He believes in himself with the same faith that people have when they kneel to statues in every corner of this Earth. Outside of himself, Weber's theology would be dangerous. These other gods are perfect. Everything they do can be justified. Everything that happens can be made to make some kind of sense. Weber is a man. He was born with the weaknesses of a man, and he will die. He has the same faith in his weaknesses as he has in his strengths. Black is just another color.

Religious men through time have spent hours and years lining up the contradictions between the world and their gods. Their imaginations are unlimited in the reconciliations and interpretations. Men have written about their gods and helped them adapt to a world that has changed dramatically. Maybe this is the intention. Maybe everything happens exactly the way God intends. I can't imagine that Weber will go to hell when he dies. God cannot be blackmailed. Not even by his own children. When Weber was sent to the rear dining room, my first reaction was violent. It seemed he had lost control of himself. It seemed the world had finally managed to wear him down. It wasn't true. Weber has given nothing and kept the wolves a room away.

November 8

Take your medicine, take your medicine. Feed it to the squirrel. Walk past the door to the rear dining room and look the other way. Weber wants a tattoo. He wants to sneak out late at night and take a cab to a tattoo parlor. There's a fat man named "Bear," he says, who can do any tattoo you choose. He works in a shack on the side of a road next to a place called Joey's Bar. I think I will go. I think I will get a tattoo. I always wanted one. I was afraid a tattoo would make it harder for people to like me.

November 9

The nights are getting cool. We are on the edge of winter. I don't doubt Weber when he says we will have no problem sneaking out to the tattoo parlor. It is obvious now that he is allowed to do just about anything he wants to do. I have seen men in suits come to visit him. I have seen students with notebooks leave his room. Gus Robinson watches everything.

The Pains of April.

Sidney Painter has agreed to go with us on tattoo night. I was surprised at first. Sidney is sensible and settled. I suppose he is sensible enough and settled enough to go to a tattoo parlor. I was in his room yesterday. While we talked, his wife sat in a chair and stared at the opposite wall. I didn't know whether to say hello or pretend she wasn't there. I pretended she wasn't there. When Sidney would turn his back for a moment I would look at her. There are times I have thanked God that my wife died when she did. Sidney's wife has Alzheimer's disease. I have seen couples with no diseases at all ignore each other with the same emptiness in their eyes as Sidney's wife, who looks at nothing. It is the nature of a relationship that it becomes less and less exciting. There are no more surprises. No more heroics. Nothing left to give or take. People lean against one another to the point where neither one can move without the other falling. So neither one moves. Exceptions are hard to find.

If you lived in a town with fifty people you might be satisfied forever to come home after work to the woman you married. There would be no other choices. But, it's not that way, and every day you can meet someone who could maybe make you happier than your wife. Every day you can meet someone that maybe you would desire more than the woman you sleep with each night. The situation becomes nearly impossible for an honest man. I suppose it is equally impossible for an honest woman, maybe more.

Just once I would like to have that feeling again. The feeling that a certain beautiful woman could give me from across the room. That curious, mischievous, sickly, animal feeling that could consume my mind to the core. Make me think about her every minute of the day. Make my imagination tie knots in my morality and piece together images of long dresses and short sentences and reds and whites and soft light browns. At times it could go much further than the flesh. There were some women that I desired simply to stand next to. There were others who I desired to control every cell in their bodies. And there were still others that I wanted to watch die from a distance. Any emotion is better than no emotion at all.

November 16

I set my clock for midnight. When the alarm went off, Gus Robinson was already getting dressed in the dark. We whispered and scurried around the room. I felt like a kid sneaking out to drink beer and look at dirty pictures. It's hard to separate the different fears. Weber slipped in the door and put his back against the wall. In the dark I could see he was wearing an old green army jacket and his baseball cap. "I called a cab from the pay phone," he said. "It'll be waiting down the block in fifteen minutes."

Gus Robinson looked from across the room where he sat on the edge of the bed tying his shoes.

He waited a minute, then sat upright and said, "I think I'll just stay here. Y'all go on without me."

Weber changed the tone of his voice.

He said, "Bullshit, Gus. Tie your shoes. If you don't go, nobody goes."

For a moment I hoped Gus would hold his ground and we could all go back to bed. I knew it wouldn't happen. We had spent several hours during the day going over and over Weber's plans. Each of us had a part to play. Sidney was the only one who laughed at the plan. He insisted that he didn't want a tattoo, but he wanted to go along for the ride. Weber's plans were detailed. He anticipated things that don't exist. He mentioned searchlights and guards in towers without a smile. Sometimes I imagine that Sidney and Weber sit alone somewhere and laugh at things I don't think are funny.

Sidney was the last one to enter the room. He carried a flashlight. When he stood next to Weber I could see that he was a much smaller man than I had noticed. We crawled out the window in a certain order. Weber

71

was the "scout." My title was "gun man." I was supposed to carry a weapon. I could feel the adrenaline beat against my chest. There were no guards and no searchlights. We walked down the block and crawled into the yellow taxi at the corner. The driver was a black man with glasses. Weber gave him an address, he started the meter, and we drove away.

"Be thinking about what kind of tattoo you want."

I hadn't thought about it at all. Truthfully, I never thought we'd actually go.

"Be thinking about the design and the colors."

I couldn't picture any design, and I couldn't picture any colors.

"Also be thinking about where you want your tattoo."

Gus Robinson was looking out the window. He said, "I'm getting mine on my arm."

I was sitting in the back seat between Gus and Sidney. Weber was sitting up front. All I could picture was pulling my pants down and having the tattoo put on my ass.

Sidney said, "My father once told me that getting a tattoo is like getting married. It seems like the right thing to do at the time." The cab driver laughed, and I spent the rest of the ride staring at the back of his head. I wondered if Weber really wanted a tattoo. I wondered if he knew the difference.

The Pains of April.

Joey's Bar had six or seven cars out front. The tattoo place next door had one red van parked on the side. I could see a light on in the room. The cab driver parked in front. We climbed out and waited for Weber to pay the man before we followed him up to the door. I started to wonder how much a tattoo would cost. Does it cost more for one design than another? Do different colors cost different amounts? Does it hurt? Does it cost less if it hurts?

"Come in!" There was one man in the room. He was bearded and fat and took up a corner. He wore cowboy boots and a gold chain and smiled the second we stepped through the door.

"Good evening, gentlemen. Come on in."

On the walls were colorful designs of all shapes and sizes. There were photographs of people whose entire bodies were covered with tattoos. The room smelled like beer. Weber talked to the man while we looked at the walls. When it was all over I had an eagle on my arm. It was the size of a fifty-cent piece and was green and red and brown. Gus Robinson had a black snake put on his forearm. The head was too big and the eyes were wrong. From the side it looked like a cartoon character. Weber had a mermaid done on his chest. He asked the fat man to make the mermaid a redhead and to give her the most perfect breasts a mermaid could have. We woke up the next day with tattoos. For weeks Sidney would laugh till he cried every time he would see the snake on Gus Robinson's arm. I spent hours looking in the mirror.

They found a sixteen-year-old boy in a neighborhood in Pittsburgh hanging from a rope in his bathroom. The newspaper article said he was found naked with pornographic material spread across the floor at his feet. Apparently he believed that by cutting off the circulation to his brain he could intensify his orgasm. He stood on the chair in the middle of his bathroom and put the rope around his neck. He bent his knees until the rope pulled tight. He tilted his head down so he could see all the pictures of the naked women laid out across the tile. Then he must have lost his balance. Maybe he heard a car door slam. Maybe the phone rang. Maybe he lost consciousness and the weight of his body snapped his neck. I imagine it took him several minutes to suffocate if suffocation was the cause of his death. When I read the story about the boy in Pittsburgh, I pictured the high school kid who works in the dining room in the evenings. Sometimes his eyes are glazed and his smile is dumb. I don't think he believes we are real. He hasn't made the connection yet between himself and us.

We are statues. We are tombstones and graveyards. We are old books with no pictures and exaggerated stories about wars and soup kitchens. The boy's name is

The Pains of April.

Brad. The boy in Pittsburgh was named Randy. I imagine that it must be harder to grow up today than it was when I grew up. Things are a long way from simple, and the world seems less dependable. Rome didn't fall in a day. It fell slowly and unevenly over hundreds and hundreds of years.

November 19

Laura Beth Snyder. She was fifteen and I was seventeen. In the afternoons she would come out and watch me play baseball. Sometimes we'd walk home together and kiss on the steps of her front porch.

"What happened to Laura Beth Snyder?"

"The same thing that happens to almost everything. My expectations got too high, and I stopped appreciating things. I stopped appreciating her. My instincts got replaced by habits. I was only seventeen. I still believed that things healed themselves. When they didn't, I believed it was her fault."

"It doesn't have to be anyone's fault."

"Yes, it does. If there's no one else to blame, I can blame God. I can blame God for making me feel guilty when I told Laura Beth after church one Sunday that I was going away to college. And I can blame God for the look in her eyes and my desire to hit her in the back of the head when she turned and walked away in her white dress. Expectations ruined the next three months of her life. Guilt is a wasted emotion. It happens too late to make a difference. I think it was meant to punish, and more than pain ever could. Someone once told me that our minds can't remember physical pain. We can remember that the pain exists, but we can't bring back the intensity or the brutal charm. If we could truly remember, women would never have a second child, and no one would find the courage to climb out of bed in the morning."

"I think maybe our minds also can't remember emotional pain. We can remember the circumstances, but we can't piece together the actual emotion."

"I think you're wrong. I think we remember emotions when we remember anything. Every image and recollection is its own emotion. You can't separate the faces and names and places from the emotions they made you feel. I also believe that it is a man's God-given right to mutilate himself in any way he wishes. It has nothing to do with his sanity."

November 25

The Pains of April.

The first time I met Laura Beth's parents was at Thanksgiving dinner. There were people in my family who had never worked hard a day in their lives. Mr. Snyder worked on a construction crew. He got up every morning, worked hard all day long, and went to bed every night at ten o'clock. His hands were large, and there were scars up and down his arms. He didn't talk much, and it was a fact that he didn't care for people who did.

Every time he looked at me I think he pictured me reaching around his daughter's back to unhook her bra. He would look away as if he could stop the action before it went too far.

Laura Beth's mother wasn't pretty. I could look at Laura Beth and then look at her mother, and it was like seeing the future. She was a short fat man with breasts. Her mustache was bigger than my Uncle Roy's.

I sat between Laura Beth and her little sister. Mr. Snyder was directly across the table. He had his wife on one side and his sister on the other. His sister lived in Alabama. She and her twenty-two-year-old daughter had come home for the holidays. The daughter was tall and beautiful. She moved like wisdom and made me feel nasty.

After dinner I sat on the porch with Mr. Snyder. I could hear the women in the kitchen washing dishes and whispering. The only word I could capture was my name. Mr. Snyder smoked a pipe. I bit my fingernails and tried to decide how I would spend the rest of my life. Twenty years earlier, Mr. Snyder had probably sat somewhere and done the same thing, except I doubt he bit his fingernails. His arms were bigger than mine, but his opportunities weren't. Laura Beth told me he had killed a man in Arkansas. I wished she hadn't told me that.

"You scared of me, boy?"

He looked straight ahead and smoked his pipe. Smoke rolled from his nose and spread out in the air. I figured there were two possible answers to his question. One was the truth and one was a lie. One sounded good and one didn't. One was easier to say than the other. I also knew that any answer was better than no answer at all. I almost waited too long.

"Yes, sir."

We sat on the porch and listened to the dishes. I know now that Mr. Snyder wanted me to be scared of him. He liked it that way. It made things simple. He always knew where he stood with a person who was afraid. He always knew where he stood with me.

The Pains of April.

Laura Beth's twenty-two-year-old cousin came out on the porch. Something changed. It wasn't a big change. It came from Mr. Snyder. The smoke rolled differently from his nose. His eyes were different. I think he was as afraid of the girl as I was of him. I don't know if he was afraid of the things she made him think, or if he was afraid of her potential to explode, or if he was afraid because she felt no fear for him. She smiled too much for people like Mr. Snyder.

She sat down next to me. I could feel Laura Beth's eyes on my back. I could hear her ears listening for the rise and fall in my sentences.

"When do you go back to Alabama?"

"Tuesday."

She looked in the same direction that Mr. Snyder looked. I'm sure they saw completely separate things. I felt good about the situation.

Then she said, "Are you and Laura Beth getting married?"

She said it like she would have said anything else. With Laura Beth listening at the screen door and Mr. Snyder an arm swing away, I knew immediately there was no right answer. Any answer would lead to another question. And the next question would be worse than the one before.

I never considered running home. It never crossed my mind to change the subject. My instinct told me to say nothing. Maybe something would happen. Maybe one of the women in the kitchen would scream in pain. Maybe a tornado would touch down in the yard. Maybe God would make a tree fall on the house.

I thought for a minute that the silence would reach into my chest and squeeze my heart dry. Then Mr. Snyder started to smile. I don't think he really wanted to, but he did anyway. He dropped his head and shook it from side to side. The girl next to me laughed, and at the time it seemed like a good thing for me to do also. Only Laura Beth still waited for an answer.

All in all it was a good Thanksgiving. I learned a lot, and the food was good. I never did get Laura Beth's bra off, and she married Wally Lutz three years later. She ended up looking exactly like her mother, and so did Wally. They had six children, and Laura Beth Snyder died of pneumonia on her fiftieth birthday. She is buried not far from my wife.

November 25

I could just sit here and wait for a vessel to pop in the top of my head and the blood to trickle down until I drown in my own fluids. Or I can sit here and

The Pains of April.

stare out the window until the contradiction between civility and animal desires begins to fester and gangrene wraps itself around my brain. If there were a woman who worried about me, she would worry now. I am quiet. She would be afraid when I got quiet. She would wonder what I was thinking. She would never guess popping blood vessels and gangrene. She would guess I was thinking about her. She would not be a separate thought. Her face would be raw in my mind.

I was a lawyer for thirty-four years. I sometimes sit and think of all my cases, and there are only a few I can still remember in detail. I had a rape case when I was a prosecutor. It was my first slap in the face. The victim was a thirty-five-year-old attractive white woman who was the wife of a rich man. Her husband ignored her. She had no children. She was bored. The accused was the son of a carpenter. He was poor and young and white and unruly. The trial lasted three days. It had nothing to do with justice. It had nothing to do with anything. If there were such a thing as justice, none of us would have been in the courtroom. I lost sight of the purpose about halfway through the trial and started making things up. There were times I wished he had killed her and covered up the clues. Instead, he penetrated her on the living room rug in the middle of a hot summer day with the windows open and his eyes closed. There were scars down his back and pieces of rolled-up skin underneath her fingernails. There was a torn bit of lace and two half-empty glasses of bourbon on the living room table. The only witnesses were God and an Irish setter named Jake. Neither one of them spoke up in time to keep the young man out of prison.

Things were not the way they were supposed to be. At a certain point the system had nothing to do with right and wrong. When a very good carpenter comes into a community, he makes the entire profession better. He raises the bar for good carpenters and puts the bad carpenters out of business. When a very good lawyer comes into a community, there can be a different result. He has the power to destroy the system itself. He has the ability to turn justice around. He can prove the innocent man guilty and set the guilty man free. He can make sense out of nonsense and have a jury laughing at the truth. Some people said I was a very good lawyer. There were times when I was very good. I was very good the day I sent that young man to prison.

In a sense, that case gave me freedom. Up until then I had believed in structure. I believed that I had certain lines to speak and motions to make in order to ensure justice. But there is no justice. It's not so easy.

I never tried heroin. I never felt the warmth rise up through my body. I never heard my blood scream for the needle. I never cried in front of my wife. When our second child was born with the body of a beast, I stood

The Pains of April.

there and stared through the glass and took long, deep breaths. She sat up in bed with the baby in her arms and thought about the sadness. All I could think about was where to hide the child.

I never understood until now that there is a difference between satisfaction and toleration. We don't get points for tolerating unhappiness. Situations don't change by themselves.

I never slept with a woman I didn't respect. Some I respected before, some I respected after. I slept with a prostitute in New Orleans on my eighteenth birthday. She turned the light on and let me look all over her body. I respected every line and tiny curve God had given her. I walked home at midnight with a different smile and her panties in my coat pocket.

I never worked on a construction crew. I never earned money with my muscles. I never looked at a building or a house and felt the pride a carpenter feels. I used to lie awake at night because my body didn't have room for the rest. I would pick at my food and rip pages out of books.

There are so many things I never did. I never traveled the world. I never shot a man. I never really figured out anything. I am more afraid of dying now than I was when I was twenty. Will I be able to hear the blood vessel pop? Will I be able to feel the blood fill my head? How long does it take?

Very soon I think the world will learn something horrible. I think it will discover something that will make us feel more insignificant than any other discovery. It will have more impact than the fact that space is endless and many of the stars we see each night burned out millions of years ago. It will make it impossible to believe that anything we could do would make any difference at all. Not everything we do, but anything. Not anything we will do, but anything we *could* do. The discovery will have people all over the world dropping their heads down into their hands. More than atoms, more than the power of the sun, more than the ten thousand miles of arteries and veins that run through our bodies. More than extinction, or the speed of light, or eyesight. It will be devastating. It will be impossible to live with.

December 2

Christmas has come and gone again. My bones feel the winter more than before. It is a dull pain that rolls in at night and keeps my feet from getting warm until morning. The great-grandchildren gave me socks. The little one stands next to his mother and keeps his big blue eyes turned away from mine.

The Pains of April.

Weber arrived dressed like Santa Claus wearing his safari hat. It was an interesting combination. The children didn't seem to notice. They only saw the Christmas lights and the big red ribbons. We had a very good time.

There was a Christmas dinner. Sidney always eats in the rear dining room so he can feed his wife. She is like a child whose body has grown old and gray. He asked me if I would like to eat Christmas dinner with them. I told him that I had already promised to eat with someone in the front dining room. I lied. I didn't want people to think I was eating in the back because I had no choice. I didn't want to sit next to someone who couldn't remember how to chew her food. Sidney knew I was lying. He is a gentle man who has learned to use his skills in a gentle way.

My daughter gave me a camera for Christmas. Later that night I held it in my hands and remembered a lesson I learned from my grandfather. I always thought of him as ancient and simple. I pictured him running his rough hands over the smooth oak tabletops until he found a spot that wasn't perfect.

I came home from college one weekend. I was taking a philosophy class, and my teacher had spent hours explaining and discussing the difference in potential between a photograph and a loaded camera. I remember the arrogance I felt when I came home and explained these things to my family using the same words the teacher had used in the classroom.

My grandfather sat in his big brown chair. I pulled the stool in front of him and placed a camera and a photograph side by side. I explained that a loaded camera has unlimited potential. Its possibilities are infinite. On the other hand, the photograph is final. It is an end in itself. It can never change. It is a single image captured and frozen. The camera has the potential to be any image, at any angle, with any shade of light. The possibilities are unlimited.

My grandfather listened to every word I said. When I had finished, he leaned forward and looked down at the camera and photograph on the stool. He picked up the camera in his hands and examined both sides. He placed the camera back on the stool and picked up the photograph. It was a picture of three soldiers standing next to an old car. The car was parked in front of a drugstore. The man in the middle stood straight and stared directly into the camera. The other men were laughing. I watched my grandfather look at the photograph. I watched his dark eyes slide across the picture the way his hands would run across the tabletops. His eyes would stop for a moment on a detail and then free themselves.

Finally he lifted his head and looked over at me. He reached out, handing me the photograph. I hadn't even looked at it before. There was a woman on the side-walk behind the car. She wore glasses and carried a dog. In the drugstore window I could see a fat man at the lunch counter. I wondered if the three soldiers were still alive. I wondered what city they had been in when the photograph was taken. I wondered what made them laugh. I wondered why I had never wondered these things before.

My grandfather saw things as they were. He saw real things in the real world. To him, the camera sat useless on a stool. It was heavy and black and metal. The photograph was alive. Each detail led to a thousand questions and a thousand answers. To my grandfather the photograph was as limitless as his imagination, and the camera was a picture that had never been painted. One existed for him, and one did not.

It was a good lesson. I looked at my grandfather differently after that. I still picture his hands searching out the rough spots across the top of a new table.

This Christmas was happy. I felt comfortable. I felt good about my family, and I felt good about my friends. Weber gave me a hug in his Santa suit and made me wear his safari hat while he handed out presents. I took pictures of all the women at the Christmas party. Mrs. Ferguson did a little dance around the Christmas tree and kissed Gus Robinson so many times I thought he might finally kiss her back. Weber managed to get slapped more than once. I don't know how he gets away with the things he does.

My daughter took me out to the cemetery later that day. It was wet and cold, but I wanted to go. We walked side by side from the road until we reached the place where my wife is buried. Her headstone is simple and clean. I have stood for hours on end and smoked cigarettes in the rain while the earth around her casket pressed against her sides. I have sat drunk in this field of dead men and tried to rub her soul into my skin.

Sometimes I wonder whether I was born to sit in a graveyard. I am a person who needs a grave to visit. At times I believe it wouldn't matter which one I picked. I would get drunk and shake my head back and forth over anyone who has ever died. Death is the cleanser. There are no more visible mistakes. No matter what terrible things you've done, everyone is allowed to die.

Betsy brought flowers. She never really knew her mother. I'm not sure what she remembers. I suppose she sits with her friends in the evenings and says what a terrible childhood she had. She's probably right. I never spanked her much. She found me drunk on the lawn one morning. When I woke up she was sitting next to me on the grass. I hit her across the face with the back of my hand.

From the cemetery I could see the house on Drury Lane. I remembered the last two years I spent there. I

The Pains of April.

was alone until Betsy hired a bullet-breasted nurse to come in the morning and leave in the afternoon. She believed she had a moral obligation to flush my cigars down the toilet and shove pills down the back of my throat. She slowly took control of my life. I could feel my fists fighting against the walls of the placenta when her fat little fingers would press into my gums. I hated the woman. Fifty years ago I would have ignored her. Twenty-five years ago I would have laughed until she went away. I hated everything she did. She would sit at the table and pick the bumps on the back of her neck until they bled.

For nearly two years I made plans to kill that woman. I pictured her eyes turning back in her head after she ate the poisoned meat. Sometimes I would take the shotgun from the upstairs closet and clean it in the kitchen. She would treat me better on those days.

She really wasn't so bad. I hated her because I had no one else to hate. It was the only exercise my mind got. I shot the refrigerator one day by accident and scared her half to death. The next morning my daughter packed my suitcase. I didn't want to come to this rest home. I hated the day I left the house. I walked through the yard like an old man. I am an old man. I look like an old man, and I smell like an old man. It seems like I've always been an old man. In the middle of springtime I remember the winter.

I have made new friends now. Some of them I like, some of them I don't. I have a new bed and a new chair. They are mine. My independence has a new form. I make my own decisions as long as they are good. It is a child's independence. There is safety and freedom in the same sentence. It exists between the open road and the rear dining room. This is where I belong.

January 4

I can sit up in bed all day and change the channels with the remote control. I can pick the scabs on my tattoo. Sometimes I don't take my pajamas off until lunchtime. The man on the TV says we have built a layer of pollution in the sky that holds in the heat like a winter coat. The world is getting warmer and warmer. Weber says I shouldn't worry about it. He says invention is the illegitimate son of necessity. The father is money. Invention is a bastard. It is a pure creation and desecration of the human spirit.

Weber gave me a list of things to worry about instead. There were ten things. They weren't numbered. He explained that each was to be worried about equally. Oatmeal and lesbianism and conspiracies. Fat women, blackjack, and unnecessary operations. Circumcision, subliminal messages, and tequila. The last thing on the list was raisins.

The man on channel eight says as the temperature rises, the polar ice caps melt. As they melt, the ocean levels begin to rise. As the ocean levels rise, we have less and less land. I kept too many commitments and broke too many promises. There are six billion people on the planet. A billion more than just ten years ago. My skin has sagged down around my face. I can see the outline of my skull in the mirror. There is a hole in the ozone layer. It lets through pieces of the sun that are dangerous. The sun has eaten my skin for nearly eighty-seven years. The same things that give life take life away. My daughter had a goldfish that ate itself to death. What a perverted instinct.

(If you could make an animal entirely from human emotion, what would it look like? It would be an eagle. The wings would be made of glass and the feathers frustrated against the body. Its eyes would be forgiveness, and its head would be sleek and unjust. I can see pride in its breast and vanity in the colors down its back. Its claws would be an ignorant mix of emotions. They would be sharp for survival, long for hatred, and strong for blind faith. They could kill a kitten in an instant or carry innocence across a nation. These are the claws that rip men's souls. They are the claws that mend the future and humiliate the past. They stand on tradition and grasp for understanding.

The beak is powerful. With power comes love. It is easy to love what the bird controls. It is easy to love the spine of the mouse. The beak is built for purpose. Its kindness exists in the restraint of this purpose. It is truth and justice and cruelty. There is no doubt. There is no hesitation. The decisions are swift, and each decision stands alone.

On the outside the eagle would be as perfect as a painting. On the inside there would be fear. There would be a million unanswered questions ignored and left to fester. There would be vulnerability and cheap security. Every organ depends on every other organ. Every vein relies on every artery, and every artery relies on every beat of the heart. The mind is left alone to survive the contradiction. The mind is left to reconcile the irreconcilable. The more knowledge it gains, the less it can ignore. The less it can ignore, the more it will struggle.)

February 19

The Pains of April.

The day before the fire was like any other day. Winter was finally over. It had begun to rain early in the morning and continued through the afternoon. Sometimes on the Gulf Coast it can rain so hard for so long that it seems it will never stop. Storms that rise from the Gulf can be as violent as a murder. Lightning splits the air, and thunder cracks an instant later and rolls away into the distance.

I played checkers with Sidney in the morning. We didn't say much. The electricity went off several times but always came back in a few seconds.

I stood at the window for a very long time. Where do all the birds go when it rains for so long? On a sunny day there are dozens and dozens of sparrows outside my window. Where do they go to stay dry?

At eight o'clock in the evening the storm got louder. I can remember the details now like a phone number. They are exact and in sequence in my mind. There was an explosion of thunder outside. The lights went out. In the darkness across the room Gus Robinson asked me if I was all right. We sat quietly and listened. The only sound was the rain coming down on the roof and running through the steel gutters.

We sat that way for about forty-five minutes. I could hear voices in the hall from time to time. Very slowly, almost the way the hands on a clock move, the sky outside became illuminated. I only noticed because I closed my eyes a moment and then opened them again. I could see the outline of Gus Robinson's features in front of the window. The features of his face looked very young somehow with the background. As it became lighter outside the rain began to die.

There was more noise in the hall. Our door swung open, and someone with a flashlight told us very calmly that there was a fire in the west wing of the building and we had to evacuate. I can recall feeling in the closet for my raincoat. The calmness of the person with the flashlight left little reason to panic.

The hallway was confusion. The beams of flashlights and emergency lights crisscrossed on the walls as people moved toward the front door and other people directed the flow. I could see when I got outside that the fire was much worse than I expected. People were standing outside on the front driveway. A light rain fell. The circling lights of police cars flashed across the front of the building. There was an ambulance, and I could see the tail end of one of the fire trucks around by the west wing.

There were several people in wheelchairs off to one side. From where they sat they could see the firemen and the other fire trucks. I didn't see Weber. I didn't see

The Pains of April.

Gus Robinson. It was dark in the shadows, and people were bumping into each other. The fire had spread from the west wing to the main building. I walked over and stood next to the wheelchairs.

The fire was spectacular. Flames lit up the sky and churned through the blue wood. Firemen held hoses and shouted to one another. I could hear windows break. I could feel the heat on my skin from a hundred yards away.

I looked down at the man in the wheelchair by my side. I had seen him several times in the rear dining room. He is blind. His face was toward the fire, and in the light I could see the blankness in his eyes. He had been blind all his life. I wondered what he pictured. I wondered what images of fire formed in his mind when he could feel the heat and hear the flames and smell the smoke. I wondered what his imagination could do with the magic of fire.

What does a blind man dream? What does a man dream if he has never seen a single sight? Does he dream smells and sounds and tastes and touches? Does his imagination try to use these things to form a face in his mind? How can he deal with colors? They have no sound, or taste, or texture. A color is a color. Green is green. It isn't blue and it isn't yellow. It isn't sour and it isn't sweet. It's green.

I looked back and forth from the fire to the blind

man. People behind me and to the side were being loaded into vans and taken to other places. It didn't seem at the time that anyone had been hurt in the fire. I didn't see in the scene around me the panic of pain or death. I remember very distinctly thinking about Sidney's wife. I remember it as a clear thought.

Weber walked up behind me and stood on the other side of the man in the wheelchair. He didn't say a word. His safari hat was gone, and he didn't seem quite awake. The three of us stared at the fire. When I looked up again at Weber, he was crying. I had never imagined Weber crying. His face was still and stern. His eyes were as blue as ever before. The man in the wheelchair couldn't hear the tears. He couldn't see the solid-gold flames. Fire is more than a color. It earns its destruction. It is worthy of the right to bring the world to its knees in the end.

We hardly slept all night. Some people were taken to hospitals, and some were taken to other rest homes. I ended up in a rest home across town with Weber and Gus Robinson. Everyone was very frightened. From the beginning there were rumors of people dying in the fire. There were numbers and names, and anyone you couldn't see was a candidate.

The next morning we woke up in a strange place. Strange people helped us, and we ate in a strange dining room. Gus Robinson was quiet. Weber came back to life. He had a captain's hat that sat up on his head like it belonged there. You could hear him laugh from across the room.

All night long relatives arrived. Betsy came to see me in the morning. She had received a phone call the night before and knew I was all right. She brought me a newspaper.

From the newspaper I learned that the fire had started in the west wing. They weren't sure yet what had caused it. Several people had suffered smoke inhalation, but only one person had died. The newspaper didn't give a name.

Later that day Weber told me the news. Our friend Sidney was the one who had died. He couldn't find his wife. He went back in to get her. She was already outside. She had already been put in an ambulance. They found Sidney's body in the doorway of their room. He suffocated in the smoke.

I had never pictured Sidney dying. He was too sensible to die. I had pictured everyone else dying, but never Sidney. When they told his wife, she only stared at the wall. I wondered if maybe she could hear but was trapped inside herself. Her eyes wouldn't cry, and her hands wouldn't wipe away the tears.

Everyone who knew Sidney liked him. He came to the rest home because he needed help taking care of his wife. He would feed her and dress her and fix her hair. When no one else was in the room he told her stories and answered the questions she couldn't ask. She was a memory to Sidney. A memory of fifty happy years. He didn't have to picture her face in his mind. He could hold it in his hands every day.

Outside the window it is a beautiful spring morning. From where I stand, there isn't a trace of the night before. April can heal itself. I can see sparrows and blue jays and white flowers in a row. The people here are very nice. One young girl has taken care of me since I arrived. She has managed to smile since late last night. Her smile seems to be authentic, but it won't go away.

My daughter brought me some clothes. The only things I saved were the pajamas on my back, a raincoat, and my briefcase. Fire consumes. If things are lost or stolen, you know that they exist somewhere. If they are burned, it is as if they never existed at all.

I can't stop thinking about Sidney. When you are old, death is never a surprise. But I am surprised. Sometimes I wish I had been the one to die in the fire. It sounds noble, but it isn't. It's selfish. Sidney was a good man.

April 4

The Pains of April.

I **woke up very early this morning.** It was still dark outside. I stayed in bed until the alarm went off. Today is the day of Sidney's funeral. It will be an open casket. His body was saved from the fire. By now it is polished and clean and dressed for the occasion. By now he looks better than he did before he died. I prefer to remember him in his underwear or laughing at Gus Robinson's tattoo.

Several people from the rest home are going to the funeral. Sidney has friends now that he never knew he had. Maybe I am one of them. People rally around the dead. The fact that they are dead usually draws more attention than anything they did while they were alive. It's part of the ritual.

We are dressed in suits. We wear ties and uncomfortable collars. The more uncomfortable we are, the more respect we are showing. There are children. Some grasp the seriousness of the occasion. At least a few understand the importance of chasing each other through the conversations. Some might remember this day for the rest of their lives. Others will pretend they do. The memory will be molded in their minds by their mothers and fathers. There is very little difference.

"Don't you remember Grandpa's funeral? Don't you remember riding to the funeral in the back seat of that old station wagon Daddy used to drive? Remember the flowers? Remember the other children? Remember walking on water and parting the Red Sea? Don't you remember anything?"

I suppose it has a lot to do with who died. The way people act differently at funerals. Gus Robinson stands alone. He has kept to himself the last few days. He checks his watch, and yawns as a disguise. There are other people here at the funeral who respond to death in the same way as Gus Robinson. Nearly everyone here feels sorry for himself. Some are sorry because they won't see Sidney again; something has been taken from them. Some are sorry because Sidney's death reminds them of their mortality. I can understand these people. I can't understand the people who cry for Sidney. If you believe in God, then you believe in heaven. If you believe in heaven, then you believe Sidney will go there. If you believe Sidney is in heaven, then it doesn't make any sense to cry for Sidney. The tears are for themselves, or they don't believe in God's heaven. They won't admit to either. It isn't necessary. It isn't necessary to push these people into a moral corner. They can believe in everything, or they can believe in nothing.

I am the perfect witness. I see everything and change nothing. My eyes see the beauty and the injustice, and

The Pains of April.

my hands stay buried in the bottoms of my pockets. I can't be blamed or given credit for any significant piece of this Earth. My body doesn't even belong to me.

When I was told of Sidney's death I felt some of the same things I felt when I first saw Weber in the rear dining room. I felt a loss of control. I felt pieces of my foundation weaken beneath my feet. It was as if each event was a necessary evil. But it wasn't either. It wasn't necessary, and it wasn't evil. We are human beings. We grow old and we die. Weber and Sidney made choices. It wasn't necessary that Sidney die when he did. It wasn't necessary that Weber end up in the rear dining room when he did. And there was nothing unnatural or evil in either case. I am the perfect witness. I have been here for as long as man has existed. I watched the apple picked from the tree and said nothing. I never tasted the sweetness, but I suffered the effects just the same. I don't apologize. Every crime needs a witness. Every miracle needs someone to give it a name.

Sidney's wife was on the front row at the funeral. We sat under a tent in the cemetery grounds. The old people and the women sat in the shade. Most all of the men stood in their suits under the sun. There was a breeze. Sidney's wife stared past the casket. She could have been a woman in shock. She could have been one of those people who ignores death. Instead, I don't know who she is. She has left her mind. I hope to God she cannot understand a word she hears. I hope she does not know what she has lost. If she can scream inside without making a noise, or if she can cry without tears, there is something cruel going on here. I watched the side of her face for a sign of anything.

During the ceremony I could hear the sounds of a Little League baseball game across the street. It was a beautiful Saturday morning. The muted cheers would go up and down in the background. As Sidney's body was lowered into the ground, I listened for the sound of bat on ball. This life is painfully long. The curtain never seems to come down. There is no time to run backstage to rest between scenes. People you love die, and the next morning you wake up. Wars are won and babies are born, and the next day you go to work. Children play baseball across the street from graveyards. Tomorrow is April 7. April 7 is my birthday. It's always been my birthday.

At the very moment that the final prayer came to an end, there was the crack of a baseball on an aluminum bat. It was a clean and clear sound followed by the roar of a crowd. The ball bounced off the center field fence, and Billy Marsh headed for second base like a bullet from a gun. Mothers and fathers and kids with Sno-Cones screamed through the fence as the center fielder picked up the ball and Billy churned towards third. The catcher took up his position at home plate waiting for

The Pains of April.

the throw. Billy's mother ran from her place in line at the concession stand. The center fielder threw the ball to the shortstop, and the shortstop turned to throw home. Billy hit the dirt, and slid headfirst at the same time the ball reached the catcher's glove. Without hesitation the umpire threw his arms out and called Billy Marsh safe at home plate.

April 6